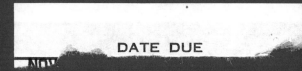

A VERY HAIRY SCARY STORY

Rick Walton

illustrated by David Clark

G. P. Putnam's Sons · New York

Text copyright © 2004 by Rick Walton.
Illustrations copyright © 2004 by David Clark.
All rights reserved. This book, or parts thereof, may not be repro-
duced in any form without permission in writing from the publisher,
G. P. Putnam's Sons, a division of Penguin Young Readers Group,
345 Hudson Street, New York, NY 10014. G. P. Putnam's Sons, Reg. U.S. Pat. &
Tm. Off. The scanning, uploading and distribution of this book via the Internet or via
any other means without the permission of the publisher is illegal and punishable by
law. Please purchase only authorized electronic editions, and do not participate in or encour-
age electronic piracy of copyrighted materials. Your support of the author's rights is appreciated.
Published simultaneously in Canada. Manufactured in China by South China Printing Co. Ltd.

Designed by Cecilia Yung and Deirdre Newman.
Text set in Badger.
The art was done with pen and ink and watercolors on
Arches 140 lb. hot-press paper.

Library of Congress Cataloging-in-Publication Data • A very hairy scary story / Rick Walton ; illustrated by David Clark. p. cm.
Summary: Upon realizing that she has stayed at her friend's house longer than she should have, Sarah decides to sneak home rather
than call her father and finds herself in a night filled with hairy, scary animals. [1. Night — Fiction. 2. Fear of the dark — Fiction.
3. Animals — Fiction. 4. Stories in rhyme.] I. Clark, David, ill. II. Title. PZ8.3.W199 Ve 2004   [E] — dc21   2002006353
ISBN 0-399- 23858-1 • 10 9 8 7 6 5 4 3 2 1 • First Impression

To Sarah,
from her very hairy scary
dad. — R. W.

To my folks, Grumps & Lalaka,
for their lifelong love and
encouragement.
— D. C.

The clock struck eight.
Sarah said, "Oh, no!
I should have been home
An hour ago!"

"No problem," Ann said,
"Just call your dad."
But Sarah said, "No,
He's going to be mad.

"If I run home
And sneak up to bed,
Dad won't know
I was here instead."

So out Ann's door

And into the night

Sarah ran to the street,

Where she turned right.

She stopped and stared

Into the black —

And thought, "Well, maybe

I should go back."

But as she turned,
She saw beside her
A very hairy scary . . .

S P I D E R !

Sarah turned
        And ran in fright,
    But then she spied
        An awful sight,

Right in her face,

Oh, no, what's that?

A very hairy scary . . .

She yelled and raced
On up the street.
But when she looked
Down at her feet,

She saw a stripe,

And her heart shrunk.

It's a very hairy scary . . .

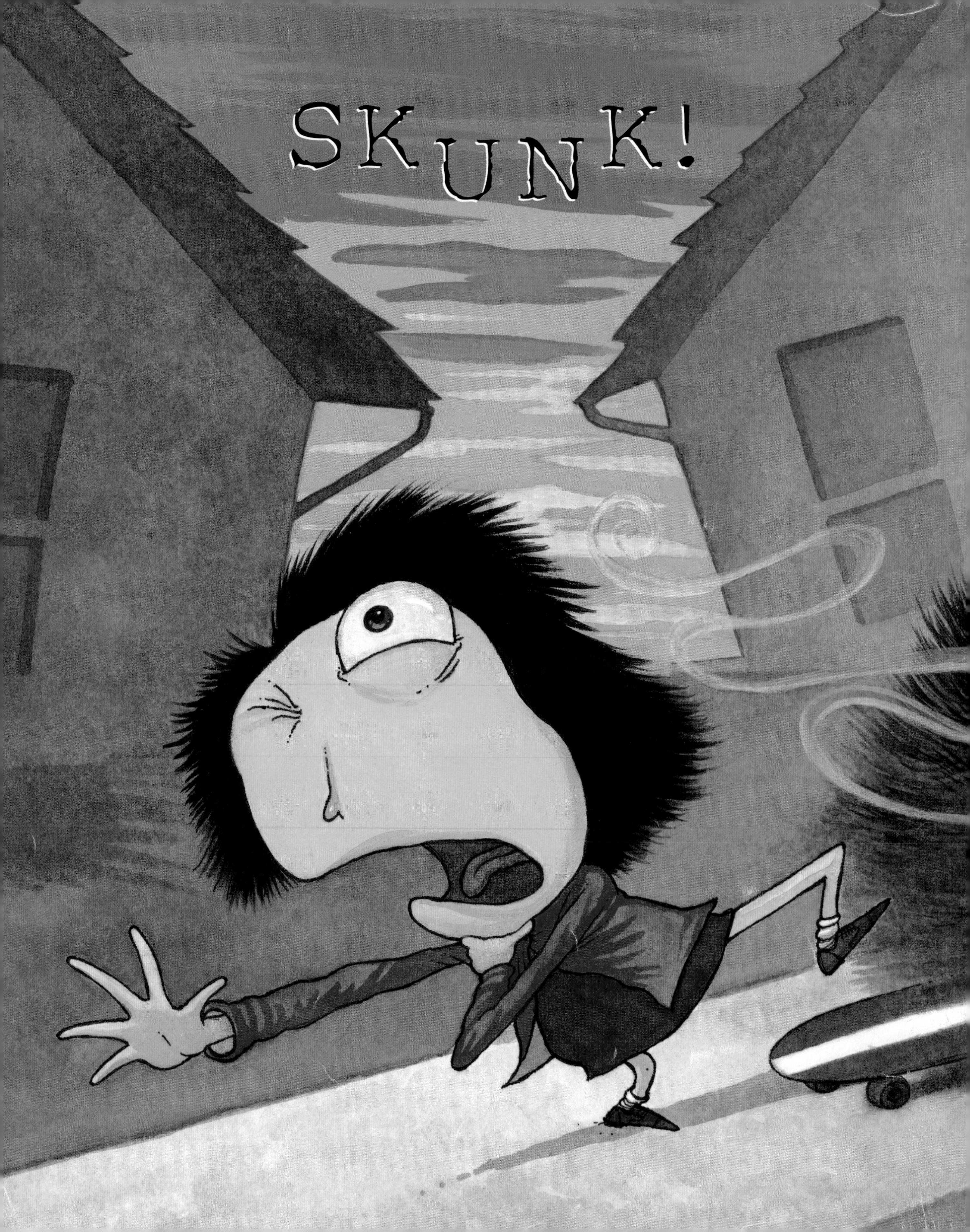
SKUNK!

"Run, feet, run!

I'm too alone!

I should have used

The telephone."

No, I can still get home,

She thought.

I'll sneak inside

And not get caught.

But at the corner,

What was there?

A very hairy scary . . .

Sarah shrieked
        And spun around,
            Up a lane
            With a bound.

Oh, no! What's blocking
        Her escape?
            A very hairy scary . . .

She turned back
The way she'd come.
Her legs were jelly,
Her heart a drum.

But there ahead,

Somethin' terrifyin'!

A very hairy scary . . .

She ran fast.

Was it following her?

Would it soon be

Swallowing her?

Sarah raced

Left and right,

Running, running

Through the night,

Until, oh, no,

This could be bad!

It's a very hairy scary . . .

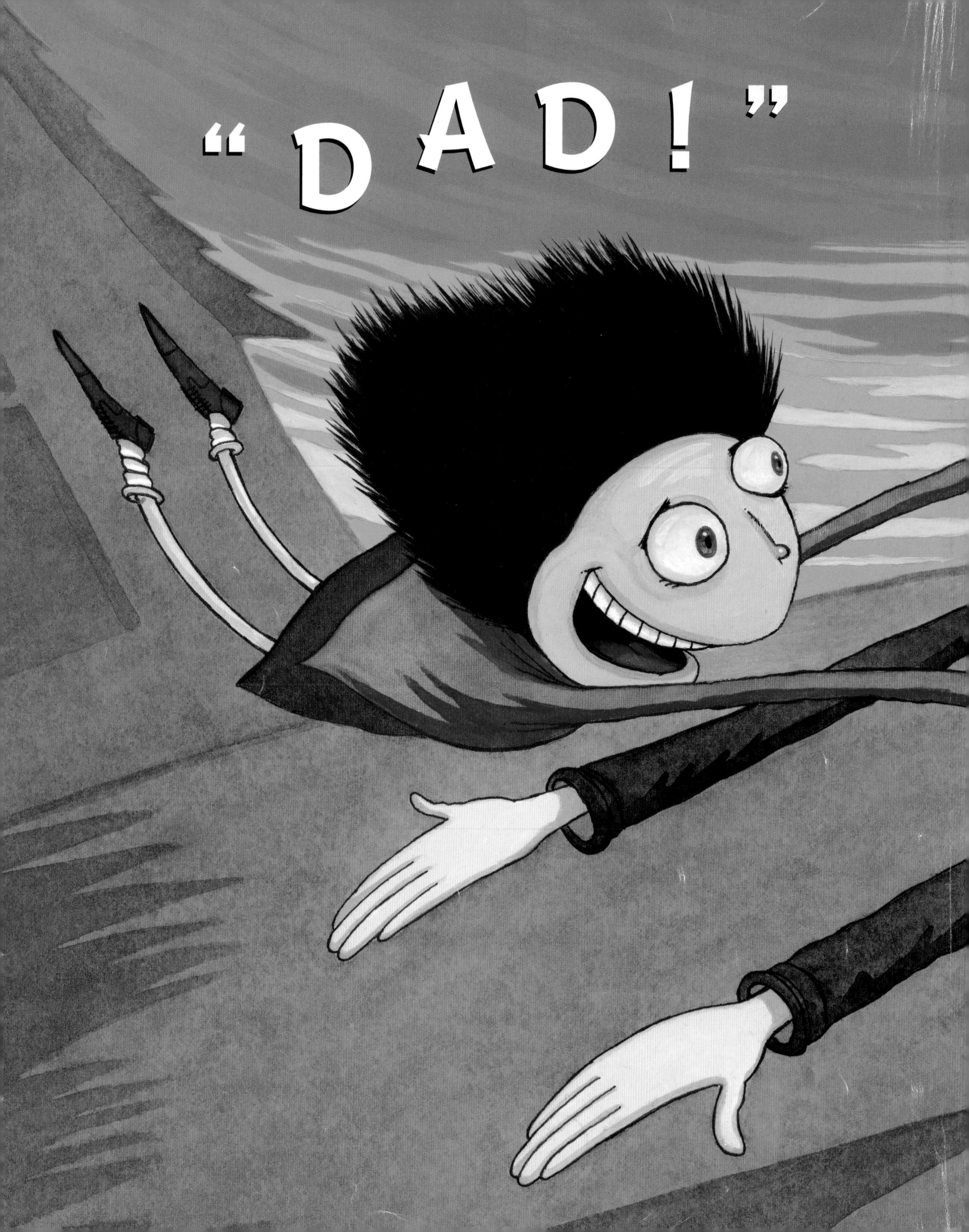
“DAD!”

Sarah shouted,
Sarah sang.
Into her father's
Arms she sprang.

"I'm sorry," she said.
"I was wrong.
I stayed at Ann's house
Much too long."

Her dad carried her,

As she hugged tight,

Through the

very

hairy

scary

night.